Little Snail Applauds

Written by Qi Zhi • Illustrated by Cheng Yue

CARDINAL
MEDIA

Little Snail was crawling on the grass.

He crawled onto a piece of newspaper and read that the Monkeys were performing that evening.

"Hi, Snail. Let's go to the show tonight, shall we?"
said Rooster. "I'm going to wear my fancy bow tie."

Snail nodded, but crawled away
wishing he had a fancy tie.

Snail crawled to the park and heard a clapping noise.

There sat Duck, clapping his feet. "Hi, Snail," said Duck. "Let's go see the Monkeys tonight! I'm going to clap loudly."

Snail nodded, but he knew he couldn't clap loudly.

Then Snail crawled up
the bamboo plant next
to his mushroom house.

There sat Sparrow. "Hi Snail. Let's meet at my house before the show tonight and we'll all go together. I'm going to cheer for them. Chirp, chirp, chirp!"

Snail nodded, but
he started to feel
sorry for himself.

Snail didn't have a fancy bow tie like Rooster.
He couldn't applaud like Duck.
And he couldn't cheer like Sparrow.

Snail was sad. He moped on the roof of his house all day. But then he had an idea.

"I don't have to be like everyone else! I need to hurry to Sparrow's house before it's too late!" Snail crawled and crawled as fast as he could.

But Snail didn't arrive at Sparrow's until everyone was already at the show. He crawled up high so he could watch the TV set below.

Snail watched the Monkeys perform and saw
Rooster, Duck, and Sparrow in the front row.

When his friends clapped and cheered, Snail thought, "Next time I won't miss the fun because I'm feeling sorry for myself. I'll just celebrate how I can!" And Snail swayed his antennae, happily.

Text Copyright © Qi Zhi
Illustration Copyright © Cheng Yue
Edited by Marie Kruegel
English Copyright © 2019 by Cardinal Media, LLC.

ISBN 978-1-64074-060-0

Through Jiangsu Phoenix Education Publishing Ltd.
All rights reserved. No part of this publication may be reproduced,
stored in a retrieval system, or transmitted in any form or by any means,
electronic, mechanical, photocopying, recording or otherwise,
without the prior permission of the publishers.

Printed in China
2 4 6 8 10 9 7 5 3 1